John J Moran

A defense of Edgar Allan Poe.

Life, character and dying declarations of the poet. An official account of his death

John J Moran

A defense of Edgar Allan Poe.

Life, character and dying declarations of the poet. An official account of his death

ISBN/EAN: 9783743347212

Manufactured in Europe, USA, Canada, Australia, Japa

Cover: Foto ©Raphael Reischuk / pixelio.de

Manufactured and distributed by brebook publishing software
(www.brebook.com)

John J Moran

A defense of Edgar Allan Poe.

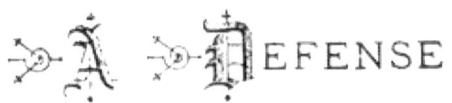

A Defense

OF

Edgar Allan Poe.

Life, Character

AND

Dying Declarations of the Poet.

An Official Account of his Death, by his Attending Physician,

JOHN J. MORAN, M. D.

WILLIAM F. BOOGHER, PUBLISHER,
1331 F Street, Washington, D. C.
1885.

Edgar A. Poe.

TO

MRS. SARAH E. SHELTON,

OF RICHMOND, VIRGINIA,

THIS LITTLE VOLUME IS

RESPECTFULLY DEDICATED.

PREFACE.

BUT for the cruel aspersions upon the character and life of America's poetic genius, EDGAR ALLAN POE, this volume would have remained unwritten.

EDGAR ALLAN POE has been more misunderstood than any other poet of the recent past. While his life was beautiful and inspired, yet aspersed, his last moments had more of sublimity than those of any of his contemporaries. The author of gems so delicate as "Annabel Lee," "The Raven," and "Lenore," while no less human and frail than others of his day, had a soul and heart that stamped him an offshoot of Divinity. In order that the story of POE's life and his last hours may be corrected and the truth made known, the following pages have been received from his learned physician, Dr John J. Moran, who attended him in his last hours and who received from the expiring poet his dying declarations, with a brief history of his life. This full and complete statement will, for the first time, be given with the hope and belief of the publisher that the truth, so long delayed, will meet with sympathy and kindness from an impartial and discerning public, will dismiss the false impressions that have been made upon the mind of his friends, will triumph over envy, error and falsehood, and the pure stream of POE's genius will flow on and on forever.

ILLUSTRATIONS.

EDGAR ALLAN POE.

THIRTY-FIVE years have elapsed since the death of EDGAR ALLAN POE. Much has been said and written in relation to this singular and most remarkable of all our poets, whose life has been an enigma to the world and whose death a mystery. The nature of his disease and how he died, up to the present day, remains a matter of doubt except so far as have been gathered from a few brief voluntary publications made by his physician. The many false charges that have been made and published, and distorted accounts that have been received as truth, have been translated into several languages; and, as Mrs. Whitman has said, in her exceedingly clear and clever little work, *Poe and his Critics*, "for ten years the great wrong done to POE by his first biographer, Rufus W. Griswold, was suffered to pass by unchallenged and unrebuked." This was true to a great extent, yet there were found two gentlemen, one of whom

knew him well, Mr. George R. Graham, of
New York, and Mr. John H. Ingram, of
London, who at a very early day after his
death (Mr. Graham in 1850, and Mr. Ingram
a few years later), wrote and published the
most forcible defense that has yet been made,
which with Mrs. Whitman's *Poe and his Critics,* have so uncovered the falsity of Griswold's
account of Poe's life that few if any are now
left to give it a place in their thoughts or
memory. This defense, however, was too
long delayed; the mind of the European
world became impressed with the idea that
the charges preferred by Griswold were true,
as they remained unanswered.

It was in 1875, when efforts were being
made by ladies and gentlemen of Baltimore
City (Miss S. S. Rice most prominent among
the ladies) to procure a monument to Poe's
memory, that I was called upon, for the first
time since his death, to give the date of his decease and the hour he died, as the monument
was ready for the inscription. At the same
time I was asked to give any incidents connected with his death, that they might be
used at the dedication. Thus twenty-six
years after his death had passed ere I was

called upon or questioned relative to the deceased poet. Without vanity permit me to say I firmly believe that had they called upon me for statements as to when he died, I could have been instrumental in preventing his dear "Muddie," Mrs. Maria Clemm, and his dear affianced, Mrs. Shelton, his first love, his "Annabel Lee," from the sore afflictions and trials and the heart-burnings that fell to their lot, and which in silence they endured. His affianced, Mrs. Shelton, wrote to me four days after his death, inquiring particularly and specifically as to how he died, the nature of his disease, and the cause. I at once replied, telling her exactly his condition, giving direct answers to her several questions, and wrote that he was as well cared for and as tenderly and faithfully nursed as he could have been by his own dear friend; that he received every attention at the hands of one of the professors of the faculty, in connection with myself, and all had been done that was possible for his best good, and that I had sent the messages left for loving friends.

In a few days I received an answer replying in these words:

DEAR SIR: I must apologize to you for having addressed a gentleman whom I had never seen and did not know. Mr. Poe was more to me than any other living being, and I write to you to learn from you, as a physician every particular in regard to his illness, disease and death, and how he died, whether conscious at any time previous to his demise or not.

As a reason for desiring to be well informed upon these points, she said that—

His enemy, his first biographer, Rev. Rufus W. Griswold, had published in *Harper's Magazine* for an article relating to his death, which I knew to be untrue, and I wished to be able publicly to deny the same over my own signature.

She further states:

I knew that Mr. Poe did not die drunk and that he was not a drunkard.

She urged me to get the magazine and see the article for myself. I did so. The article ran thus:

Edgar Allan Poe is dead. **Thousands will hear of it,** but none will regret it. He died in an unknown, out-of-the-way hospital in the city of Baltimore, in a fit of *delirium tremens.*

Her predictions were true to the letter, as you will learn further on in this memoir. His death occurred on October 7th, 1849. These letters were written, received, and answered inside of three weeks after his death. This lady who took such interest in Mr. Poe was his affianced the second time, and was living at her home in Richmond, Va., last June twelve months ago. I paid her a visit,

the particulars of which will be found in this volume. Time speeds on and I repeat that thirty-five years have passed, and at this late period I am invited and urged to make known the facts so long desired in reference to his death. I am grateful to a kind Providence for having spared me to give the positive facts and unfold to the public mind much that has not been made known, and I hope to remove all doubt in respect to the uncertainty which has so long surrounded this part of Poe's history and life. I now proclaim to the world that he has been shamefully abused and misrepresented, that the habit of intemperance, which to some extent did cling to him in his earlier history, did not continue with him in his more mature life, and that what I shall record, shall be a true, unvarnished story from personal intercourse for sixteen hours during his last illness, from his death-bed statements, from information received elsewhere, and from near and dear friends, those who knew him and loved him.

It was my sad duty as his physician to sit by his death-bed: to administer the cup of consolation: to moisten his parched lips; to wipe the cold death-dew from his brow; and to catch the last whispered articulations that fell from the lips of a being, the most remarkable, perhaps, this country has ever known. Let me entreat your thoughtful attention, therefore, to a plain, unvarnished story of a checkered life, and the strange and melancholy events that darkened the last hours of a dying genius. There is no heart so dead to human sympathy as not to feel some degree of interest in the deceased poet, whose wonderful gifts have long been acknowledged, not only in this country, but wherever polite literature is known, and in regard to whose death so many incredible stories have been told, and so many absurd and cruel misstatements have been made. Some, indeed, are left who feel for him in the highest degree. Some are not here, but elsewhere, who feel with an intensity unknown to earth, but realized only in the bright realms above, where the father's prayer and the mother's tears have touched the Mighty Heart whose throbbings move the universe.

It is proper that I should state that the work I have undertaken, at the earnest entreaties of his numerous friends, is not of my

seeking, profoundly impressed as I have
been by the conviction of duty I owe to the
memory of the deceased and to his numerous
friends as well. Yet I was reluctant in yield-
ing my consent to undertake so responsible
a task. But now, after frequent appeals
made to me from time to time by many of
the leading journalists and literary men of
this country, and by earnest, sympathizing
ladies, whose sensitive hearts are ever touched by human misfortune. and who are
always in advance of the sterner sex. I am
persuaded that I should lend my feeble aid
as a witness to the truth, and refute the foul
accusations cast upon the memory of Poe.
and repel the vile slanders respecting his
death. The time has come when every fact
and incident of his remarkable career should
be made known. But of all these entreaties,
none have done more to determine my purpose than those of the lady to whom he was
affianced, and his dear mother-in-law, Mrs.
Maria Clemm. These appeals, made years
ago, have never lost their influence, though
seemingly unheeded in the lapse of time.
They come back to me with renewed force,
especially since the interest manifested in

New York, a few years ago, by friends whose admiration of the poet led them to undertake the erection of a suitable monument to perpetuate the memory of this wonderful genius.

All praise to the names of Gill, Winter, Campbell. Abbey. Palmer, Stoddard, and others in New York, and to Dr. Elmer R. Reynolds of Washington City, and others; but I accord equal commendation to the generous and sympathizing ladies who have jointly and heartily united their efforts to accomplish what the men alone could not do.

All praise to Madame Dion Boucicault, Madame Phillips. Mrs. Bellew, Mrs. Crosby, Mrs. Coleman. Mrs. Dahlgren. Mrs. Wm. Astor, and others.

LOWELL, *March 2, 1850.*

DR. JOHN J. MORAN.

DEAR SIR: I think you will pardon the liberty I take in again writing to you. But first permit me to most gratefully thank you for your kind letter relative to the death of my beloved (son) E. A. Poe. In November last I received a letter from Neilson Poe, saying that you had placed in his possession my son's trunk, and asking me in what way he was to dispose of it. I instantly replied to him requesting him to send it on to me, that *I alone* had *any claim* to it. I was anxious to receive it, as the publishers of my son's work are constantly writing to me for the lectures and other papers which, we all think, must have been in his trunk. At all events procure from him my darling Eddie's letter to myself, which I sent to him to convince him that I was entitled to the trunk, and inclose them to me, for they are a thousand times more precious to me than rubies. Will you do this great favor for me? Have you seen the March number of *Graham's Magazine?* If not, do get it and read the noble defense of my son by Mr. Graham. I shall be most anxious for your reply; and may God bless you for soothing the dying hours of my own precious Eddie. Most gratefully, MARIA CLEMM.

I repeat the language of Mrs. Clemm. One of her letters to me opens with these words: "May God bless you for soothing the dying hours of my precious Eddie." Then she urges me to accept two of his letters written to her, that I might use them in his defense. These two letters were sent to her just before his death. "Use them," she writes, "in defense of his character and name; they testify the truth: they are to me a thousand times more precious than rubies." The tear-stained letter which was written to me shortly after his death is with me now upon my person, as a talisman and shield for my defense in this conflict with his enemies and accusers, many of whom are able writers and journalists of the present day. They have written without a knowledge of the facts, thereby doing great injustice to his memory. Her appeals have stirred my soul to its deepest depth, and given me a longing desire to do what I could, even at this late day, to relieve the public mind of the false impressions made regarding Poe's habits of life; how he died, the nature of his death, his true condition at that period, and to give the parting words uttered in the last moments of his life. I do not design to arraign any writer, nor to prefer charges against biographers. I have been somewhat reflected upon by at least one of these, in regard to my knowledge of mental diseases, and especially that class of subjects who suffer from intemperance and frequent debauches.

The hospital in which the poet died has been questioned as to its standing and character. My professional experience has been assailed, my veracity and even my own identity have been disputed. You will not accuse me of egotism or self-praise. As a stranger to you, you have a right to demand and to know who I am, whether I held the position of resident physician at the Washington University Hospital in the city of Baltimore, where the poet died; whether he died in my charge, and what was the character of the institution named. Concerning an oft-repeated slander, I here affirm that Edgar Allan Poe did not die under the influence of any kind of intoxicating drink.

Remembering the mother's blessing, and the tears and entreaties of the broken-hearted affianced, Mrs. Sarah E. Shelton, who yet lives, and who said to me a few months ago, at her home in Richmond, "I would have gone down to my grave in the firm belief that Mr. Poe did not and could not have died a drunkard or from drink." I now undertake to make good this declaration.

The hospital in which Poe died was second to none in Baltimore as to size, comforts and location. It was known for many years as the *Washington College University Hospital*, in which hundreds of students daily traversed its wards, receiving instruction at the bedside of patients from able professors of the faculty. It contained two hundred beds, and had seldom less than one hundred and fifty patients, whose names were on the hospital record. I have the honor to say that I conducted and controlled this institution for six years as resident physician, living with my family on the premises. I had the entire charge and responsibility of house and patients, including United States sailors, a portion of the hospital being set apart for this class of patients, who were sent there by order of the Government.

Just after the death of ´Edgar Allan Poe, before the lifeless corpse had become cold in the grave, an enemy, *an avowed and personal enemy*, and who became his administrator and was his first biographer, made haste to write and publish the foul calumny and falsehood that Edgar Allan Poe died from *delirium tremens* at some *unknown and out-of-the-way hospital* in Baltimore City, and which Mr. George Graham pronounced "an immortal infamy" and declared it to be dastardly and false, and "nothing but the fancy sketch of a perverted, jaundiced vision;" and strange to say this man's work, Griswold's *Memoir of Edgar Allan Poe*, though repeatedly denied upon the best authority, continued to be much sought after, and its poisonous effects are yet seen and felt on both continents.

I have entered upon this work fully prepared, with living testimony, legally indorsed, in proof of all that I shall say in relation to the life, character, and death of the poet. I am frank to acknowledge that much that I shall say will not be new in regard to his family history. I shall repeat much that has been written by able writers, but I desire, and shall endeavor to give credit to such authorities as I shall quote, and hope to introduce many facts and incidents that have not been generally known. I have in my possession much that will be publicly made known for the first time. These come from the nearest relatives, given to me by those who were nearest and dearest to him, and from one who loved him as she did her own life.

Mr. David Poe, the great grandfather of EDGAR ALLAN POE, with his family resided in Baltimore and was engaged in mercantile business. During the Revolution Mr. David Poe became a deputy quartermaster of the Maryland line, and had often been called Major and sometimes General Poe. He occupied for his quartermaster's office a part of the old building on Baltimore street, near Charles, which was, a few years ago, occupied by Armstrong. Cater & Co. The building was owned by Poe, and it was at this office that he received *General* **Lafayette.** *Count Rochambeau, Count DeGrasse* and other French officers. When the troops of our revolutionary ally, General Lafayette, were in this vicinity, long after the French had departed, cuirasses or breast-plates of metal and bridle-bits of lignum-vitæ wood were found in the cellars of the buildings, and were prized as souvenirs of the war. In this connection it may be interesting, as a scrap of history connected with the Poe family, to state that in *Niles' Register*, October 23, 1824, is recorded a visit of the nation's guest, General Lafayette, to Baltimore, in which the following grateful remembrance appears:

After an introduction of the surviving officers and soldiers of the Revolution who resided in and near Baltimore to the General, he observed to one of the gentlemen present, "I have not yet seen, among these gentlemen, my friendly and patriotic commissary." The General was informed that Mr. David Poe was then dead, but his widow was still living. He expressed an anxious wish to see her. Said the General: "Mr. David Poe, who resided in Baltimore when I was here, had, out of his own very limited means, supplied me with five hundred dollars to aid in clothing my troops, and his *wife*, with *her own hands, cut out* 500 *pairs of pantaloons, and superintended the making of them for the use of my men.*"

The *Register* further states that when the good old lady heard the intelligence she shed tears of joy, and the next day *was visited by the General, whom* she most *gladly received, and the visit was most gratefully appreciated*, &c. The General, on his visit to Mrs. Poe, was escorted by a company of horse, and spoke in grateful terms of the kind and friendly assistance he had received from herself and husband. "Your husband," said he, pressing his hand upon his breast, "was my *friend*, and the aid I received from you both was most beneficial to me and my troops."

Mr. David Poe, Jr., son of Gen. David Poe. of revolutionary memory, was the father of EDGAR ALLAN POE, who was born in Boston on January 19, 1809. The citizens of three respective cities have claimed for themselves his place of birth, viz.: Boston, Baltimore and Richmond. But it is generally conceded and believed that Boston is entitled to the credit and honor of POE'S having drawn his first breath in that city. Very soon thereafter his parents removed to Richmond. General Poe designed his son David, the father of Edgar, for the law, and placed him in the office of Wm. Gwinn, Esq., Baltimore, for the prosecution of his studies; but while a student he became fascinated with a beautiful young English actress whose name was Elizabeth Arnold. So devotedly attached was he to this charming young woman, that when little more than eighteen years of age he eloped with her and was married. He was disowned by his parents for this unwarranted step. He soon adopted his wife's profession and went on the stage. In a few months after their marriage, and after the birth of their first child, the parents of David relented, and the young couple returned to their paternal home, where they were cordially received. The time allowed for acts of kindness and sympathy towards these erring children was of short duration.

Soon after their return to home and favor of father and mother they left the paternal roof to follow their profession, and started for Richmond, Va. In 1815 the youthful parents of POE died within a few weeks of each other, from consumption, leaving three children, Henry, EDGAR, and a daughter named Rosalie, unprotected and unprovided for. On the death of their parents EDGAR, though a mere child, was adopted by Mr. John Allan, a wealthy citizen of Richmond, who was childless and whose wife became passionately fond of the beautiful and attractive child. It was mainly her love for the boy that led to his adoption by Mr. Allan, whose name he gave to EDGAR. EDGAR ALLAN POE was but six years old when adopted. He was a very pretty child and noted for his precocity. Mr. Allan was fond of the boy and treated him as if he were his own son. Scarcely had the little orphan time to become acquainted with his new parents, before he was carried by them to Europe. It was in this wise, in 1816, that the Allan family visited England on matters pertaining to business, taking with them their adopted son. After traveling through England and Scotland, they placed him at the Manor-house school in Church street, Newington. He was placed under the care and instruction of the Rev. Dr. Bransby, whom the poet so quaintly describes in *William Wilson*, which is considered one among his best stories. Friendless and orphaned as he was, he spent a happy, if not the happiest, part of his life in this sombre English village. Here POE remained for nearly five years, and to this sequestered spot he looked back in after life with feelings of pleasure and great satisfaction, if not with pride; and to the training and direction given there to the bent of his mind, his scholarly acquirements are chiefly attributed.

In 1821 he was recalled by his adopted parents, and placed by them at an academy in Richmond, where the Allans resided. The boy was now but twelve years old. Mr. Allan had by this time become so much attached to Edgar that he was petted and apparently spoiled, as his every wish was gratified; but these generous acts did not spoil him, but left him with an unnatural sensitiveness to affection toward those who desired his best good. It was at this early period that he manifested his gentleness and docility. He was willing and eager to be taught, and exhibited a kind and humane disposition toward all. Toward the dumb brute, as he says of himself, "my tenderness of heart was so well known as to make me the jest of my companions." This tenderness of heart and generous nature increased with his growth and strengthened with his strength, and its beauty and fullness were developed in after life.

In 1822 Mr. Allan placed Edgar at the University of Charlottesville, Va. Here the Rev. Dr. Griswold, the writer to whom I have before referred, began his attack. He charges Poe with having been dismissed from the university for habits of intemperance and other vices. I am pleased to say that these false charges have been fully refuted by the president and secretary, William

Wertenbaker, of the faculty, whose testimony, over their own signatures, I now produce. Mr. William Wertenbaker, the secretary, indorsed by the president, Dr. Stephen Maupin, as being worthy of confidence, says in his letter of reply to the charges made: "There is nothing on the records of the faculty to the prejudice of Poe. He spent one entire session at the university. At no time did he fall under the censure of the faculty, and he was not known to be addicted to the use of stimulants." This much is history authenticated and published in his memoirs and confirmed by Dr. G. White to me in person a few months ago in Richmond. He said to his friend Dr. White, "You are acquainted with the character of the gentlemen with whom I am daily associated; you know them to be gentlemen, well educated and highly esteemed. Their habits are to take a glass of toddy two or three times a day, and occasionally to be intoxicated. I have, at long intervals, participated and have sometimes felt its effects, but I paid the penalty by four or five days in bed. I could not become a dram drinker, it would have soon killed me." His sensitive nature could not

endure it.   His mother-in-law. Mrs. Clemm,
has said that a cup of strong coffee would
intoxicate him.   Dr. Whyte remarked to me,
"I never knew POE to gamble or get drunk.
We all played cards for pastime and amuse-
ment, and we sometimes drank wine, but
never got drunk or gambled for money."
The Doctor was a student with POE at
Charlottesville that session.

It is not my purpose to follow in detail
POE's history, but I design to give a brief
review of his habits of life in respect to his
indulgences in the intoxicating glass, so that
you may be better able to determine in your
minds whether he was the debauchee and low
character as charged so frequently by his
enemies.   I do not wish you to understand
me as saying that Mr. POE never drank ardent spirits in his early manhood, or that he
was never under its influence, but I hope to
be able to so strengthen your belief in the
character of his life and habits as well, that
you will unite with me in declaring against
the wholesale abuses and reiterated slanders,
as a tissue of gross untruths originating in
the brain of a designing enemy.   In the latter part of his life, four years previous to his
death, he was perfectly temperate.

Leaving to his biographers the years that intervene, I introduce him again in 1829. In this year he returns to his foster-father's home, in Richmond, in the latter part of March, but too late to see the familiar face and receive the smile of welcome from his foster-mother; she was buried the day before his return.

Of this melancholy visit the poet himself says:

> I reached my home, my home no more,
> For all had flown who made it so;
> I passed from out its mossy door,
> And tho' my tread was soft and low,
> A voice came from the threshold stone
> Of one whom I had earlier known.

Edgar deeply felt her loss and mourned her death, causing him to express to Mr. Allan a wish for the military profession, in the hope of being sent away from home. Mr. Allan gratified his desire, and by his influence secured him a position in the Military Academy at West Point. The records of that institution show that EDGAR ALLAN POE was admitted July 1, 1830.

The rigid rules, regulations, and restraints of the Academy were not in accord with the freedom he had hitherto enjoyed. He re-

mained but a short time under their control,
and returned to Mr. Allan's house once more,
where he was kindly received and where he
remained some length of time, long enough,
in fact, to engage himself in a matrimonial
alliance with the love of his childhood, Miss
Royster, now Mrs. Shelton, of Richmond.
She was a sweet young lady in her teens, and
he but two years her senior. She was his
beautiful "Annabel Lee," and lived at Richmond, his "kingdom by the sea." Let the
poet speak for himself of this early love:

ANNABEL LEE.

It was many and many a year ago,
    In a kingdom by the sea,
That a maiden there lived whom you may know
    By the name of ANNABEL LEE;
And this maiden she lived with no other thought
    Than to love and be loved by me.

I was a child and *she* was a child,
    In this kingdom by the sea;
But we loved with a love that was more than love—
    I and my ANNABEL LEE;
With a love that the winged seraphs of heaven
    Coveted her and me.

And this was the reason that, long ago,
    In this kingdom by the sea,
A wind blew out of a cloud, chilling

My beautiful ANNABEL LEE;
So that her highborn kinsmen came
And bore her away from me,
To shut her up in a sepulchre
In this kingdom by the sea.

The angels, not half so happy in heaven,
Went envying her and me—
Yes!—that was the reason (as all men know,
In this kingdom by the sea
That the wind came out of the cloud by night,
Chilling and killing my ANNABEL LEE.

But our love it was stronger by far than the love
Of those who were older than we—
Of many far wiser than we—
And neither the angels in heaven above,
Nor the demons down under the sea,
Can ever dissever my soul from the soul
Of the beautiful ANNABEL LEE;

For the moon never beams without bringing me dreams
Of the beautiful ANNABEL LEE;
And the stars never rise, but I feel the bright eyes
Of the beautiful ANNABEL LEE;
And so, all the night-tide, I lie down by the side
Of my darling—my darling—my life and my bride,
In the sepulchre there by the sea,
In her tomb by the sounding sea.

When Mr. Allan became aware of this engagement, he was very angry and did all in his power to prevent its consummation, chiefly on account of EDGAR's youth.

A quarrel ensued and the poet, unable to submit to what he considered unjust and

arbitrary treatment by Mr. Allan, left the
house with the intention of offering his services in aiding the Poles in their struggles
against Russia. Many accounts are given as
to where he went. A recent biographer
assumes to have ascertained that he entered
the United States Army under the assumed
name of Edgar A. Perry; but my own impression is that he never designed to be
remote from his first love, his "Annabel
Lee." and many circumstances warrant this
opinion. His brother Henry's action may
have given rise to this report.

It was only last summer, during an interview with Mrs. Shelton, that I learned from
her the strength of the attachment between
the poet and herself—in plain words, how
much they loved. She talked freely with
me of their childhood and riper years when
they were in each other's company. She
named the street where her father lived,
and said that EDGAR ALLAN POE'S foster-
parents lived in the house on the opposite corner. "We spent much of our time together
when we were children. A few years after
Mr. Allan built a large mansion farther up
the street, about four squares from where

we stand." She seemed to be thoughtful and musing, when I remarked, "You met again in the years when you began to know more of the realities of life." She said, "Yes, but you will excuse me. I am lost in wonder and amazement at the singular drama now being enacted. Oh, sir, you can have no idea of the thoughts that have so crowded upon my memory and occupied my mind. How often I have wished to see his physician, so that I could learn from his own lips Mr. POE's dying words. And to think that so many years after his death, we are face to face, reviewing his life, from his childhood to his grave. All this I have anxiously hoped for before I should die, and it is now fulfilled." The venerable lady then put her handkerchief to her face and wept. I spent four hours in her company, in talking of POE's decease, comparing notes and gathering important facts to aid in my defense.

This interview with one immortalized by the poet's song I shall never forget. Our sympathies were in unison, and I am not ashamed to confess that it was with difficulty that tears were restrained. I am happy to say that Mrs. Shelton is yet living, and though in feeble health and well advanced in years, her face indicates a peaceful mind and a joyous hope of the rest beyond.

Poe left Richmond, it is true, but doubtless with the hope of one day returning again, to take to his bosom the idol of his heart. Years intervened, but her image never left him, waking or sleeping. It is certain that he put himself in a position as near to his heart's desire as was discreet, to learn something regarding her and his foster-parent. He learned too soon the sad tidings that fell like a nightmare upon his sensitive nature, and palsied his heart and gave a death-blow to all his hopes and fond anticipations. He learned that Mr. Allan had married a young woman, the beautiful Miss Patterson, whom he well knew, and that the love of his youth, Miss Royster, to whom he had plighted his affections, had married a gentleman of wealth in that city, named Shelton.

This was a severe blow to the ardent young poet. Disappointed and dejected, unfortunate in almost everything he had previously undertaken, many less sensitive in their natures would have resorted to the bowl for relief. Not so with the distressed poet.

Relying upon that innate spirit of indepen-
dence which possessed his soul, he determined
now to devote his whole mind to literature for
his support. He sought and received encour-
agement by his active brain and the use of
his never-failing pen.

In the year 1833 he is again brought promi-
nently before the public as a competitor for
two prizes offered by the proprietor of the
Saturday Visitor, published in Baltimore
City, for the best prose story and the best
poem. The poet wrote and sent to the committee selected to award the prizes six of his
stories and the poems of the Coliseum. The
committee, composed of eminent professional
and literary men, after a critical examination of a mass of papers received from numerous contributors, decided unanimously
that POE, to them unknown, was entitled to
the premiums and that he richly deserved
them.

Not contented with this award, the adjudi-
cators went out of their way to draw up and
publish the following flattering critique on
the merits of the writings submitted by POE:

Amongst the prose articles were many of various and distinguished
merit but the singular force and beauty of those sent by the author of
the " Tales of the Folio Club " leave us no room for hesitation in that

department. We have, accordingly, awarded the premium to a tale entitled the "MS. Found in a Bottle." It would hardly be doing justice to the writer of this collection to say that the tale we have chosen is the best of the six offered by him. We cannot refrain from saying that the author owes it to his own reputation, as well as to the gratification of the community, to publish the entire volume, "Tales of the Folio Club." These tales are eminently distinguished by a wild, vigorous and poetical imagination, a rich style, a fertile invention, and varied and curious learning.

Signed

JOHN P. KENNEDY.
J. H. B. LATROBE.
JAMES H. MILLER.

Mr. Kennedy, chairman of the committee, became the firm friend of Poe and continued so to be until his death, and when informed of the decease he declared it impossible to credit any of Griswold's stories of the poet's life.

In 1834 Mr. Allan died, leaving his adopted son no part of his great wealth. In 1835 Poe engaged with a Mr. White, of Richmond, who had commenced the publication of the *Southern Literary Messenger* in that city. His former friend, Mr. Kennedy, urged Poe to send something to the *Messenger* for publication.

Poe did as he was desired by Mr. Kennedy, and it so pleased Mr. White that he spoke of it in the highest terms in the next number of his periodical.

Poe's reputation grew so rapidly that Mr.

White gave him a position on the editorial staff of the *Messenger*, at a salary of one hundred guineas per annum. In order to give his entire attention to the duties assumed, he removed to Richmond, where the magazine was published. During the year 1836 Poe was fully installed in his new relation to the *Messenger*.

It was in Richmond, among his own kindred, that he met his "Lenore," his cousin, Virginia Clemm, the daughter of his father's sister, Maria Clemm. She reciprocated his affections, and to her he was married. She was very young in years, and from predisposition was soon to be the victim of pulmonary disease. It had already seized her for its prey, but the ardent and sincere attachment for his choice was irresistible, and with but little of this world's goods and a small income he married his cousin. Under other circumstances a better help-meet could not easily have been found, or one better calculated to make his life a happy one.

In 1837 Poe left the *Messenger* to assist the proprietors of the New York *Quarterly Review*, a work for which his scholarly acquirements rendered him eminently qualified. It is proper to state that Mr. White parted with POE very reluctantly, without a word of complaint, and with no accusation of intemperance, as charged by Griswold.

POE removed to New York with his family and resided on Carmine street, and up to this period of his life I have brought the subject of my lecture without one charge of intemperance made by his accusers, or other charges that have not been disproved by the clearest testimony given by those who knew him personally and well.

I will take the liberty of presenting additional witnesses to testify to his good character. I am permitted to introduce the Hon. Richard Hengist Horne, of London. I quote his own language:

A few leading features only can be sketched. No cunning barrister preparing an important brief; no great actor studying a new part; no analytic chemist seeking to establish the fact of a murder by discovery or proof of blood or poison in some unexpected substance; no Dutch painter, working for months on the minute finish of all sorts of detail, in the background as well as the foreground of his picture, ever took more pains than EDGAR ALLAN POE in the production of most of his principal works. Let no one attempt to imitate POE without his genius and acquirements. The copyist would be discovered and denounced in an instant.

Let me introduce a gentleman of learning and character, a citizen of New York, Mr. William Gowans, whose testimony is in direct confirmation of the fact that POE was not addicted to the use of intoxicating drink. He said:

I will give you my opinion of this gifted but unfortunate genius. It may be estimated as of little worth, but it has this merit, it comes from an eye and ear witness, and this, it must be remembered, is the highest legal evidence. For eight months one house contained us and one table fed us. During that time I saw much of him and had an opportunity of conversing with him often, and I must say that I never saw him the least affected by liquor, nor ever descend to any known vice. He was one of the most courteous gentlemen and intelligent companions that I have met during my haltings and journeyings through divers divisions of the globe; besides he had an extra inducement to be a good husband, for he had a wife of matchless beauty and loveliness, and temper and disposition of surpassing sweetness and was as much devoted to him and his every interest as a mother is to her first-born.

This gentleman boarded with Mrs. Clemm until she broke up housekeeping. He had every opportunity to know the habits of POE.

I wish now to introduce the testimony of Mrs. Osgood, a distinguished lady, to show his extreme kindness and affection for his wife. She remarks:

It was at his own simple yet poetical home that the character of the poet appeared in its most beautiful light—playfully affectionate, witty, and at times wayward as a petted child. For his gentle and idolized wife and for all who came he had, even in the midst of his most harassing duties, a kind word, a pleasant smile, grateful and courteous attention. At his desk, beneath the romantic picture of his beloved "Lenore," he would sit hour after hour, patient, assiduous and uncomplaining, tracing in exquisite penmanship, and with almost superhuman swiftness, the lightning thoughts, the rare and radiant fancies as they flashed through his wonderful and ever-wakeful brain.

If there is any place where a man can be seen in his true light and where his true character is fully displayed, it is at his own home.

In 1838 POE removed to Philadelphia, where he was engaged as a contributor to the *Gentlemen's Magazine* of that city. His talents soon produced brilliant effects, and in May, 1839, he was appointed to the editorial management of that periodical. Towards the close of 1840 Mr. George R. Graham, owner of the *Casket*, acquired possession of the *Gentlemen's Magazine*, and merged the two publications in a new series known as *Graham's Magazine*. Mr. Graham was only too willing to retain the services of the brilliant editor, and found his reward in so doing.

POE, aided by the liberality of his employers, in a little while increased the number of subscribers to the magazine from five to fifty thousand. He continued in this capacity until near the close of 1842, at which time POE resigned the position of joint editor of *Graham's Magazine*.

In 1843 the *Dollar Magazine* offered a hundred-dollar prize for a story, which was awarded to POE for his tale of "The Gold Bug."

In 1844 the poet moved to New York, whither his increasing fame had already preceded him, and where he now entered congenial society and a fairer and better field for the recognition of his literary abilities. It is generally conceded that the first journal for which he wrote in New York was the *Mirror*, a daily paper, holding the position of sub-editor and critic. The paper at that time belonged to N. P. Willis and Gen. George Morris. During the whole six months that Poe was engaged on the *Mirror*, Mr. Willis asserts that he was invariably punctual and industrious, and daily at his desk from nine in the morning until the evening paper went to press. At this period some of Poe's most remarkable productions appeared, including "The Raven." This poem first appeared in *Colton's American Review* for February, 1845. It was also printed in the evening *Mirror*, with the author's name attached, and in a few weeks was known throughout the United States and in Europe.

His name and fame were at once carried across the water, drawing warm eulogies from some of the first poets and critics of the old world. For this masterpiece of genius, which Mr. Ingraham declares has probably done more for the renown of American letters than any single literary performance, Mr. Poe received the pitiful sum of ten dollars. It has been stated that he composed "The Raven" while in a fit of *delirium tremens.* In refutation of the falsity of this charge, I have the testimony of a lady of intelligence and literary culture, the wife of a distinguished General, formerly of New York, who assures me that Poe composed "The Raven" while at her father's house in that city. It was his habit when he left the house to leave the manuscript in the old iron safe belonging to this lady's father. She declares he was never known to taste anything intoxicating while he was at her father's house. She lived at home and saw Poe every day.

In July, 1845, the entire control of the *Broadway Journal* was confided to Poe. Its owners having limited capital and less talent it soon came to nought. During his control of the *Broadway Journal*, Poe's labors were great and extremely severe: enough, indeed, to destroy the brain of almost any other man. He made it, while under his management, the best cheap literary paper that was published at that day. In the winter of

1845-'46, Mr. Poe was a favorite in the literary circles of our great commercial metropolis, as was also his young and beautiful wife. His love and devotion to his wife, to which I have already referred, was a sort of rapturous worship. Of this charming feature of Poe's character, Mr. Graham says:

I have seen him hovering around her when she was ill, with all the fondness and tender anxiety of a mother for her babe. Her distressed cough would cause him a shudder—a heart chill that could be seen. It was this hourly anticipation of losing her that made him a sad and thoughtful man, and lent a mournful melody to his undying song. It was for his dear wife's sake that Poe left the city of New York. Ill health, want of worldly knowledge, a sick and dying wife to distract him, all combined to overpower his efforts, and for her sake and to secure for her peace and quiet, he left the busy, bustling city, retired to a small Dutch cottage in the quiet town of Fordham, Westchester County, New York. Here he passed with her the three remaining years of her life.

It was in the summer of 1846 that Poe removed his dying wife to the quietude of Fordham. Here I desire also to quote the language of Mrs. Whitman to corroborate the statements already made regarding Poe's habits, gentleness, and sincere devotion to his wife. Mrs. Whitman had frequently visited his wife at their peaceful home, and she says:

The noblest memorial yet raised to his memory was his undying devotion to his dear "Lenore." There in loneliness and privation, through many solitary hours, in the bleak and dreary days and nights of January, 1847, he watched her failing breath.

Till at length, one day in that cheerless month,

An angel came from the blest afar
To bear her deathless spirit through the golden gates ajar.

The dear wife of his bosom had passed away, and in some slight degree I did realize his distress of mind and sorrow of heart in his own dying words as I held his hand at his death-bed. He cried out in language so pathetic, with heart all torn and bleeding, "Oh, my dear Lenore, my dear Lenore! how long before I shall see my dear Virginia!" impatient to depart and be with her at rest.

The poet's grief for his lost wife was so great that he became very melancholy and reticent: moving about the house in apparent listlessness and indifference. This state of mental distress lasted for weeks, but through the kind attentions and encouraging words of his dear "Muddie," as he called his mother-in-law, Mrs. Clemm, he gradually regained his wonted vigor of mind and body and resumed his work. With no companion but Mrs. Clemm, he remained at his quiet home, musing over the memory of his lost "Lenore," and thinking out the crowning work of his life.

Here he remained for one whole year, gradually receiving friend after friend, and devoting his best energies to the completion of his "Eureka." At the close of this, the most immemorial year of his life, he wrote his "Ulalume."

Early in 1848 he determined to make an effort once more to start a magazine of his own. To raise funds for this purpose he announced his intention of delivering a series of lectures in the places where he had the greatest number of intimate friends, hoping to receive from them subscriptions to support his enterprise. The place at which he designed and where he expected to obtain his largest support was Richmond. He issued a prospectus and started North, delivering his first lecture in the library of the New York Historical Society. He lectured also in Boston and Lowell. Not obtaining the necessary number of subscribers to start his journal on a solid basis, he abandoned the enterprise, returned to Fordham and resumed work on his "Eureka."

In the summer of 1849 he again visited Richmond, his former visit having been for the purpose of engaging in business with a new firm, in which a lady was interested, one whom he had known in former years and who was in possession of means sufficient to successfully establish a magazine. She was now a widow.

The first visit was in the month of October, 1848. Whether by accident or design I do not know, but I do know, as I received it from the lady herself a short time ago, that it was during that visit to Richmond that she saw him, for the first time, since she had become a widow, and that it was in the autumn of the year and the month of October, 1848, that he first met her since he had become a widower. In the summer of 1849 POE took final leave of his home and friends at Fordham. These were the friends who stood by him during his severest trials and afflictions, among them being his mother-in-law, Mrs. Clemm. She had been his guardian and guide, and had cared for him as only a mother could do. I give the statement of one of his truest friends and nearest neighbors, and one who, with his family, was more intimate with him than almost any other, being together for more than four years, as additional evidence in refutation of the stories and calumnies charged against POE. I allude to Mr. S. P. Lewis.

Mr. Lewis says:

My wife and I often visited him during the last illness of his wife, and waited for her funeral; and when POE finally took his departure for the

South, the kissing and hand-shaking were at my front door. He was hopeful, we were sad, and tears gushed in torrents as he kissed his "Muddie" and my wife "good-bye," Mrs. Clemm predicting a final adieu.

Mr. Lewis continues:

POE was one of the most affectionate and kind-hearted men I ever knew. I never witnessed so much tender affection and devotion as existed in that family of three persons. I have enjoyed the most closest intimacy with Poe, and never saw him under the slightest influence of any stimulant whatever. He was, in truth, a most abstemious and exemplary man. Our acquaintance was made in the year 1846, and continued until the summer of 1849, when he left for the South.

This gentleman gives a candid and truthful account of POE for four years, from 1845 to 1849.

Allow me here to present to you the declaration and earnest appeal made to High Heaven, in the most solemn manner, by POE, in a letter to a personal friend, and at the time and in the face of these calumnious charges. I refer to his letter to Dr. Snodgrass, of Baltimore, recently published in the *Baltimore American*. He said to the Doctor:

I now thank you for your defense of myself as stated. You are a physician, and I presume no physician can have difficulty in detecting the drunkard at a glance; you are, moreover, a literary man well read in morals; you will never be brought to believe that I could write, as I daily write, as I wrote it, if I were a drunkard. In fine, *I pledge you, before God, the solemn word of a gentleman,* that I am temperate even to rigor; nothing stronger than water ever passes my lips. I have now only to repeat to you in general, my solemn assurances that my habits are as far removed from intemperance as the day is from the night. My sole drink is water. Will you do me the kindness to repeat this assur-

ance to such of our own friends as happen to speak of me in your hear-
ing?   I feel that nothing more is requisite, and you will agree with me
on reflection.

(Signed)   EDGAR ALLAN POE.

I here aver that there is no evidence and
never has been, that Poe ever was seen
drunk, or that he ever got drunk from the
year 1845 to 1849, embracing a period of
four years.   Later he confesses to the effect
of stimulants at long intervals, but of these
four years preceding his death, we have the
clearest testimony that he was a temperate
man.

He was a member of a temperance associa-
tion, at Richmond, and delivered two lectures
upon the subject in that city, to each of
which his "Annabel Lee" accompanied him,
as she did to all other lectures delivered by
him in that city.   After he had been in
Richmond a few months, it was rumored he
was to be married to Mrs Shelton, his "Annabel Lee," to whom he was engaged in his
youth, when she was Miss Royster.   I have
the testimony from the pen of the lady herself, written to me thirty-two years ago, of
the fact, and from her own lips in June last,
that she was engaged to be married to Poe
at the time of his death.   Mrs. Shelton declares that he was the most courteous gentle-

man she had ever known; that no one could be in his company and not be benefited by it, and above all that he was super-sensitive to a fault at anything that would, in the most remote degree, offend a lady. He inspired all with whom he had business intercourse or dealings of any kind with an affectionate esteem, such as you would feel for a near friend or a dear relative.

I feel that I have trespassed too long upon the kind forbearance of my readers in this brief history of the poet. I may have been tedious in the presentation of so large an amount of testimony in refutation of the false charges made against his good name, and the only apology I can offer is the interest I feel in my theme and my desire to secure a generous judgment. Is it not impossible for one who labored so assiduously with brain and pen, by day and by night, through all the disastrous circumstances surrounding him and the misfortunes that fell to his unhappy lot, to produce those masterpieces which fill bulky volumes, poems of exquisite beauty, stories of weird and fascinating splendor, and critiques that are in all respects among the finest in our literature, and these productions, amidst the drudge ries of editorial routine, on periodicals and weekly papers, at times when he was physically exhausted by watching over the bedside of his dying wife, whose life was one long disease? Is it possible, I ask, that a drunkard could have done all this? No, no. The constancy of his labors and the demand upon his brain and time, up to a short period before his death, at which time he produced the crowning work of his life, his "Eureka," forbid the supposition. But if to take a glass of wine or brandy with convivial friends, at long intervals, which he confesses to have done and to have felt its effects in his earlier manhood, is to brand a man with the name of "drunkard," blast his character and reputation. I say to his revilers and persecutors, "Let him that is without sin cast the first stone." Until then let the death slumber of EDGAR ALLAN POE be quiet in his tomb, and let his ashes rest in peace. But have these cruel calumnies fallen upon the unfortunate poet alone? No. Many of his friends have felt them most keenly. One yet lives, now in her seventy-third year, who loved him in life, sympathized with him in his afflictions, wept and mourned for his untimely death, and with grief and tears of sorrow will go down to the grave lamenting the sad fate of him who was dearer to her than life itself. She has suffered and felt, as only a pure and sensitive woman can feel, not only her great loss, but the cruel and unjust assault upon the memory of him she loved.

In closing this part of my narrative, I am constrained to ask your indulgence while I present some remarks of Mr. George Graham in defense of POE. I do this at the request and earnest desire of Mrs. Clemm, and in compliance with a promise made to her years ago. Mr. Graham says:

For three or four years I knew POE intimately, and for eighteen months I saw him almost daily; much of the time writing or conversing at the same desk; knowing all his hopes, as well as his hard struggle with adverse fate; yet he was always the same polished gentleman, the quiet, unobtrusive, thoughtful scholar, the devoted husband; frugal in his personal expenses, punctual and unwearied in his industry, and the soul of honor.

The poet himself made this solemn declaration to a personal friend: "By the God who reigns in heaven, I swear to you that my soul is incapable of dishonor. I can call to mind no act of my life which would bring a blush to my cheek."

I come now to the closing scenes of the life of the long-lamented and deceased poet.

It is with the last sixteen hours of his life
that I have especially to do. This is my
mission and the duty I am called upon to
perform. They are the hours that have been
shrouded with so much mystery, and in regard to which so many false statements have
been made.

After twenty-five years I was called upon
as his physician. I was supposed to know at
least the date of his decease, and as a monument was about being placed to his memory
in Baltimore it became necessary that I
should be consulted. I was applied to for
the necessary date. I cheerfully gave it, and
the same was cut upon the monument so
creditable to the ladies and gentlemen whose
philanthropic hearts moved them to secure
this memorial to the genius and worth of
the dead poet. It is hoped that if I was sufficient authority for this record, that I may
receive corresponding confidence from my
readers in the statements I make.

Permit me to ask at your hands the confidence you would give to any respectable
physician making a statement respecting a
deceased patient who was in his care for
sixteen hours before his death. I cannot but
believe that you will accord this measure of

confidence to one who saw, handled and watched over his patient, cared for him, conversed with him. and received his dying statement.

I have stated to you the fact that Edgar Allan Poe did not die under the effect of any intoxicant, nor was the smell of liquor upon his breath or person. He was in my care and under my charge for sixteen hours. He was sensible and rational fifteen hours out of the sixteen. He answered promptly and correctly all questions asked, spoke freely, and made certain statements, and gave certain directions to whom I should write, and a confession of what related to himself, his mother-in-law, and the lady to whom he was to have been married. He told me, in answer to my questions, where he had been, from whence he came, and for which place he started when he left Richmond, when he arrived in Baltimore, and the name of the hotel where he registered. from which I received his trunk before his death. The names of the ladies to whom he requested me to write were given. and their answers to my letters after his death came speedily and are with me now.

It has been charged that Poe was made

drunk and then "cooped," and voted a number of times at an election held in Baltimore
about that time. This charge I unhesitat-
ingly deny. One word will demonstrate its
falsity. That election was held October 3d,
the day before POE left Richmond, and he
was not in Baltimore until October 5th. He
was brought to the Washington College University Hospital on October 6, 1849, about
9 o'clock A. M. and died between 12 and 1
o'clock on October 7th.

His biographers all agree that he left Richmond on October 4th, but affirm that when
he landed in Baltimore he was caught, cooped,
drugged, voted, and then turned upon the
streets to die; that some one saw him who
knew him and brought him to the hospital
at night in an unconscious state, and that he
died before morning with inflammation of
the brain, being insensible until his death.
It is true that POE left Richmond on October
4, 1849, not by train but by boat. There
was no railroad from Richmond to Baltimore.
I have the evidence and the proof from Mrs.
Shelton, his affianced, that the poet parted
from her at her residence at 4 P. M. October
4th, to take the steamer "Columbus" for Baltimore, intending to visit Philadelphia and

New York, to close up some business he had with certain publishers and return to Richmond in a few days. She states that when he said "good-bye," he paused a moment as if reflecting, and then said to her: "I have a singular feeling, amounting to a presentiment, that this will be our last meeting until we meet to part no more," and then walked slowly and sadly away. What a sorrowful prophecy was there in those parting words, and how fearfully was it fulfilled.

Of the first meeting and the last farewell, the illustrious poet sings in his wonderful poem, "Ulalume:"

The skies they were ashen and sober,
  The leaves they were crisped and sere;
It was night in the lonesome October
  Of my most immemorial year.

Our talk had been serious and sober,
  But our thoughts they were palsied and sere,
  Our memories were treacherous and sere,
For we knew not the month was October,
  And we marked not the night of the year.

Then my heart it grew ashen and sober,
  As the leaves that were crisped and sere,
  As the leaves that were withering and sere,
And I cried, it was surely October,
  On this very night of last year,
  That I journeyed, I journeyed down here

It was in October that he first saw her

when a widow; it was on October 4th that he
left, to see her face no more on earth; and it
was on October 7th when he died.

The boat arrived in Baltimore about 4
o'clock on the morning of October 5th.   It
landed at its dock on the corner of Pratt and
Light streets.   Poe started for the hotel on
Pratt street, north side, opposite the Philadelphia depot, called "Bradshaw's," now
" The Maltby House."   A colored man from
the boat went with him and carried his
trunk.   He left for Philadelphia about noon
and went as far as the Susquehanna River,
across which the passengers had to be trans-
ferred by boat, there being no bridge at that
time.   The river being very rough, owing to
a storm then blowing. Poe refused to venture
across.   He remained on the cars and returned to Baltimore.   Arriving there at
about 8 o'clock P. M., a porter carried his
trunk to the hotel he had left in the morning.
Alighting from the cars he turned down
Pratt street, on the south side, and walked
toward the dock where his boat was.   He
was followed by two suspicious characters,
as the testimony of the conductor will show,
and when he reached the southwest corner
of Pratt and Light streets, he was seized by

the two roughs, dragged into one of the many sinks of iniquity or gambling hells which lined the wharf. He was drugged, robbed, stripped of every vestige of the clothing he had on when he left Richmond and the cars a little while before, and reclothed with a stained, faded, old bombazine coat, pantaloons of a similar character, a pair of worn-out shoes run down at the heels, and an old straw hat. Later in this cold October night he was driven or thrown out of the den in a semi-conscious state, and feeling his way in the darkness, he stumbled upon a skid or long wide board lying across some barrels on the west side of the wharf, about thirty yards from the den. He * * * fared as did one of old. He had fallen among thieves, who stripped him of his raiment and departed, leaving him half dead. He stretched himself upon the plank and lay there until after daybreak on the morning of the 6th. A gentleman passing by, noticed the man and on seeing his face recognized the poet. He called a hack, and giving the driver a plain card with my address, and on the lower right-hand corner the name of Poe, the poet was carried to the hospital, arriving there about 9 o'clock.

I had him placed in a small room in the turret part of the building where patients were put who had been drinking freely. The room can be recognized in the cut by the star. He was clad in the shabby suit I have described, and being unconscious I had him put in the place indicated, not knowing at that moment the cause of his distress. I now know that he was perfectly sober when he returned to the city.

My witnesses are Judge N. Poe, of Baltimore, a second cousin of the poet; and the conductor of the train, Capt. George W. Rollins, well-known in Baltimore. The following testimony was given to me by the conductor a few days after the poet's death: Meeting him on the street he said, "I saw in the papers the death of the gentleman I had on my train the other day." I asked, "Do you know who he was?" He said he did not at that time, but he had learned since that it was EDGAR POE. He remarked that he was the finest specimen in appearance of a gentleman that he had lately seen. "I was attracted to him from his appearance." I said, "Captain, how was he dressed?" He replied, "In black clothes; his coat was buttoned up close to his throat. There were two men

well dressed that came aboard of the train
from the other side of the river, having come
from Philadelphia or New York. They took
a seat back of POE. From their appearance I
knew they were sharks or men to be feared,
and when I got out of the train at Baltimore
I saw them following POE down towards the
dock." I asked the conductor if POE was in
liquor. "Why," said he, "I would as soon
have suspected my own father." I then related to him the facts regarding POE and
where found the next morning, and he expressed his thorough belief that those two
men went through him. A similar statement was given by this conductor to Judge
Nielson Poe sometime during the same
month of the year 1849, and was repeated
to me by Judge Poe last April two years
ago while sitting in the court-room, after
the court had been dismissed. We spent more
than an hour discussing the poet's life and
death.

And just here let me give you the words
of Mrs. Shelton, who yet lives, regarding the
style of clothing he had on when he left her
in Richmond on the 4th of October. I asked
Mrs. Shelton how he was dressed. She replied, "In a full suit of black cloth;" remark-

ing that he always wore black clothing, and was very neat in dress and person. "Had he a watch or jewelry on his person?" She could not say, as he always wore his coat well buttoned up to his throat, covering much of his person. I said, "He told me his contemplated visit to New York was on business, and that he expected to return in a few days." I related to her the facts of his case, where found, how dressed when brought to the house, and she instantly exclaimed, with tears in her eyes, that he was robbed, as I have always believed, and drugged to accomplish it. When brought to the hospital, as I have said, he was unconscious. I had him disrobed and made comfortable in bed. I placed an experienced nurse at the door of his room to preserve quiet, to watch over him and to notify me when he showed signs of waking. He was, at that time, in a heavy sleep or stupor. I left him and on entering my office below, I discovered the hack still standing before the entrance door of the hospital, as you will see in the cut. I asked the driver, "What are you waiting for?" He said, "My hire." I asked, "Who sent you here?" He replied, "You have the ticket," meaning the card he had brought with him.

I asked. "Where did you find this man?"
"On Light street wharf, sir." I said, "Dead
drunk, I suppose?" He replied. "No, sir; he
was a sick man, a very sick man, sir."

"Why do you think he was not drunk?"
I asked.

"He did not smell of whiskey," said the
driver. "he is too white in the face. I picked
him up in my arms like a baby, sir, and put
him in the hack."

Without further delay I paid the man his
fee. Little did I then think that after thirty-
five years I should be called upon to give a full
account of Poe's death and to defend the man
whom I at that hour believed to be drunk :
and that man, the great American genius,
whose name is now a household word.

In a few minutes Poe threw the cover
from his breast, and looking up asked the
nurse, "Where am I?" The nurse made no
reply but rang for me. I attended the call
immediately, and placing my chair by the
side of the patient's bed, took his left hand in
my own and with my right hand pushed
back the raven locks of hair that covered his
forehead. I asked him how he felt. He
said, "Miserable."

"Do you suffer much pain?" "No."

"Do you feel sick at the stomach?"   "Yes, slightly."

"Does your head ache, have you pain there?" putting my hand upon his forehead.

"Yes."

"Mr. POE, how long have you been sick?"

"Can't say."

"Where have you been stopping?"

"In a hotel on Pratt street, opposite the depot."

"Have you a trunk or valise or anything there you would like to have with you?" supposing he had other clothing than that which he brought on his person to the hospital.   He said. "I have a trunk with my papers and some manuscripts."   Note this, there was no clothing in the trunk.   A new suit of wedding clothes was to have been placed in it for the groom.   His visit was a business one and was to be a short one.   I offered to send for his trunk.   He thanked me and said, "Do so at once;" remarking, "Doctor, you are very kind."

I sent the porter of the house with an order for his trunk, which was brought in less than an hour.

The sick man said, "Where am I?"

"You are in the hands of your friends," I

replied, "and as soon as you are better, I will have you moved to another part of the house, where you can receive them." He was looking the room over with his large dark eyes, and I feared he would think he was unkindly dealt with, by being put in this prison-like room, with its wired inside windows, and iron grating outside.

I now felt it necessary that I should determine the nature of his disease and make out a correct diagnosis, so as to treat him properly. I did not then know but he might have been drinking, and so to determine the matter, I said, " Mr. POE, you are extremely weak, pulse very low ; I will give you a glass of toddy." He opened wide his eyes, and fixed them so steadily upon me, and with such anguish in them that I had to look from him to the wall beyond the bed. He then said, "Sir, if I thought its potency would transport me to the Elysian bowers of the undiscovered spirit world, I would not take it."

"I will then administer an opiate, to give you sleep and rest," I said. Then he rejoined, "Twin sister, spectre to the doomed and crazed mortals of earth and perdition."

I was entirely shorn of my strength

Here was a patient supposed to have been drunk, very drunk, and yet refuses to take liquor. The ordinary response is, " Yes, Doctor, give me a little to strengthen my nerves." I found there was no tremor of his person, no unsteadiness of his nerves, no fidgeting with his hands, and not the slightest odor of liquor upon his breath or person. I saw that my first impression had been a mistaken one. He was in a sinking condition, yet perfectly conscious. I had his body sponged with warm water, to which spirits were added, sinapisms applied to his stomach and feet, cold applications to his head, and then administered a stimulating cordial. I left him to sleep and rest. He slept about one hour. When he awoke, I was again summoned to his bedside. I found his breathing short and oppressed, and that he was much more feeble. I saw that his life was in great danger. He asked several questions as to where he was, and how he came there. Remarking in answer to my question as to where he went after he returned from the Susquehanna, he said that he had started for the boat, "I remember no more," said he, "but a vague and horrible dread that I would be killed, that I would be thrown in the dock."

I said, "Mr. POE, you are in a critical condition, and the least excitement of your mind will endanger your life; you must compose yourself and remain quiet."

He said, "Doctor, I am ill; is there no hope?"

"The chances are against you."

"How long, oh! how long," he cried, "before I can see my dear Virginia, my dear Lenore!"

I said to him, "I will send for her or any one you wish to see." I knew nothing of his family or friends, and supposed the persons to whom he referred might live in the city, or that his family might live there.

I asked him, "Have you a family?" "No," said he, "my wife is dead, my dear Virginia. My mother-in-law lives; oh! how my heart bleeds for her. She had forebodings of this hour, and said when we last met and parted at Fordham, 'Eddie, I fear this will be our last meeting.'"

He loved his mother-in-law with no common love, as his poetic words declare:

TO MY MOTHER.

Because I feel that, in the heavens above,
  The angels, whispering to one another,
Can find, among their burning terms of love,
  None so devotional as that of "Mother."
Therefore by that dear name I long have called you—
  You who are more than mother unto me,
And fill my heart of hearts, where death installed you,
  In setting my Virginia's spirit free.
My mother—my own mother, who died early,
  Was but the mother of myself; but you
Are mother to the one I loved so dearly,
  And thus are dearer than the mother I knew
By that infinity with which my wife
  Was dearer to my soul than its soul-life.

I said, "Mr. Poe, I will send for or write to any one you desire me."

"Doctor," said he, "Death's dark angel has done his work. Language cannot express the terrific tempest that sweeps over me, and signals the alarm of death. Oh, God! the terrible strait I am in."

"Shall I write to any one for you?"

"Yes, Doctor, write to my mother-in-law and Mrs. ——no, too late! too late!"

Then he said, "Write to both at once; write to my mother-in-law and tell her 'Eddie is here'——no, too late! Doctor, I must unbosom to you the secret of my heart, though dagger-like it pierces my soul. I was to have been married in ten days."

He wept like a child, and even now I can see his pale face that told too plainly the depth of grief he felt, and the large tear-drops forcing their way down the furrows of his pallid cheeks. I again asked, "Shall I send for the lady?"

"No, write to both: inform them of my illness and death at the same time, and say that no conscious act of mine brought this great trouble upon me. How it has happened that I am brought to this place, God only knows. My mind has kept no record of time: it seems a dream, a horrible dream."

I said, "Mr. POE, my carriage is at the door; I will send for the lady."

"No," said he, "write to Mrs. Sarah E. Shelton, Richmond, Va., and Mrs. Maria Clemm, Lowell, Mass."

Beef-tea and stimulants had been freely given and kept up at short intervals. I remained by his side, watching every breath and movement of his muscles. He had no tremor or spasmodic action at this period, which was twelve hours from his entrance in the hospital. I noticed the color deepening upon his cheeks and forehead, blood vessels at the temple slightly enlarging. I ordered ice to his head and heat to his extremities, and waited in his room about fifteen minutes longer, observing no change except an increase in the circulation. His pulse, which had been as low as fifty, was rising rapidly, though feeble and variable. I left him for a short time, to attend to other patients in the house. I had sent for his cousin. Mr. Nielson A. Poe, now Judge Poe, of the orphan's court of Baltimore, having learned that he was related to my patient: and also for a Mr. Herring and family, who lived in the neighborhood. Judge Poe came as soon as notified and also the Misses Herring. These were the only persons who called to see him until after his death.

Poe continued in an unconscious state for half an hour, but when roused he was conscious. On visiting him again I found his pulse feeble, sharp, and very irregular. I took my seat by his bedside and closely watched him for twenty minutes at least; the pupils of his eyes were dilating and contracting. Death was rapidly approaching.

Just at this moment my friend, Professor J. C. S. Monkur, one of the oldest physicians of the faculty, and who gave to me much of his time at the hospital, came into the sick chamber. As soon as he fixed his eyes upon the patient he said. "He will die; he is dying now." After a careful examination, Dr. Monkur gave it as his opinion that POE would die from excessive nervous prostration and loss of nerve power, resulting from exposure, affecting the encephalon, a sensitive and delicate membrane of the brain. He advised the continuance of the remedies, including the beef-tea and stimulants. I saw the patient lifting his hand to his mouth as though he wanted a drink: I put a small lump of ice in his mouth, and gave him a sip of water from a glass, to ascertain what difficulty, if any, he had in swallowing. He drank half a glass without any trouble. He seemed to revive a little and opening his eyes, he fixed them upon the window. He kept them unmoved for more than a minute. I have, since that time, been forcibly impressed with the wild fancies in that wonderful poem, "The Raven." Did he hear a "gentle tapping at the window lattice," and was his heart still a moment, "this mystery to explore"? Did he see that stately raven "perched upon his chamber door? Perched, and sat, and nothing more."

The dying poet was articulating something in a very low voice, and at length he spoke more audibly and said, "Doctor, it's all over." I then said, "Mr. Poe, I must tell you that you are near your end. Have you any wish or word for friends?"

He said, "Nevermore."

At length he exclaimed: "O God! is there no ransom for the deathless spirit?"

I said, "Yes, look to your Saviour; there is mercy for you and all mankind. God is love and the gift is free."

The dying man then said impressively, "He who arched the heavens and upholds the universe, has His decrees legibly written upon the frontlet of every human being, and upon demons incarnate."

I then consoled him by saying, "He died for you and me and all mankind. Trust in His mercy."

How impressive are his words in "The Raven:"

Is there—is there balm in Gilead?—tell me—tell me, I implore!

THE RAVEN.

* * * * *

Open here I flung the shutter, when, with many a flirt and flutter,
In there stepped a stately Raven of the saintly days of yore.
Not the least obeisance made he; not a minute stopped or stayed he,
But, with mien of lord or lady, perched above my chamber door—
Perched upon a bust of Pallas just above my chamber door—
     Perched, and sat, and nothing more.

* * * * *

But the Raven, sitting lonely on that placid bust, spoke only
That one word, as if his soul in that one word he did outpour
Nothing farther then he uttered; not a feather then he fluttered—
Till I scarcely more than muttered "Other friends have flown before—
On the morrow *he* will leave me, as my hopes have flown before."
     Then the bird said "Nevermore."

* * * * *

"Prophet!" said I, "thing of evil!—prophet still, if bird or devil!—
Whether Tempter sent, or whether tempest tossed thee here ashore,
Desolate yet all undaunted, on this desert land enchanted—
On this home by Horror haunted—tell me truly, I implore—
Is there—*is* there balm in Gilead?—tell me—tell me, I implore!"
                           Quoth the Raven, "Nevermore."

                    *   *   *

And the Raven, never flitting, still is sitting, still is sitting
On the pallid bust of Pallas just above my chamber door;
And his eyes have all the seeming of a demon's that is dreaming
And the lamp-light o'er him streaming throws his shadow on the floor;
And my soul from out that shadow that lies floating on the floor
                           Shall be lifted—nevermore!

I here add my testimony to the fact that Poe did recognize the one Supreme Being, who holds in His merciful hand the destiny of all.

Hear his own deathless words:

"Father, I firmly do believe—
I know, for death who comes for me
From regions of the blest afar,
Where there is nothing to deceive,
Hath left his iron gates ajar;
And rays of truth you cannot see
Are flashing thro' eternity."

The glassy eyes rolled back; there was a sudden tremor, and the immortal soul of EDGAR ALLAN POE was borne swiftly away to the spirit world.

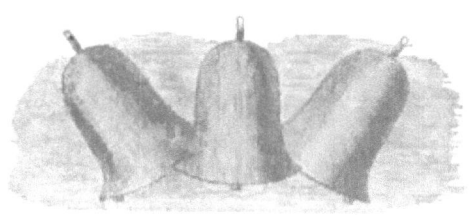

TOLLING BELLS.

The bells! Ah, the bells!
The heavy iron bells!
Hear the tolling of the bells!
  Hear the knells!
How horrible a monody there floats
  From their throats—
  From their deep-toned throats!
How I shudder at the notes
  From the melancholy throats
  Of the bells, bells, bells—
    Of the bells.

NOTE.—The original draft of the poem, "The Bells," when first published contained eighteen lines, eleven of which we select for our purpose, being appropriate and significant. We are enabled so to do by the courtesy of Mr. John W. Sartain, who published the original poem as it was first written.

After Poe's death his body received the usual care and attention. He was clothed with a suit of black, a white cravat, and a collar about his neck. It may be of interest to the readers to know how this suit of black was obtained. I therefore take pleasure in recording the facts and giving credit to whom credit is due. A resident student at the hospital named George McCalpin, from Alabama, gave the pants; Albert Grey, a student from Leesburg, Va., gave the coat: the writer a vest, neckcloth, etc. His coffin was a plain one. To hide it from the gaze of his numerous visitors and to avoid unpleasant criticism, my wife, with a few ladies in the neighborhood assisting her, made a very neat muslin covering for it. This was spread over it and the body laid thereon. At night its folds served as a covering for his person. The coffin, as I have said, was a plain one, simple in structure, void of cushion for his head, and without lining, plated handles, or plate for his name. The material of which it was made was not what it appeared to be. It represented walnut, but it was not; it was simply a poplar coffin, stained to imitate walnut. I was not able then, out of my limited means, to furnish a better one. This

I paid for out of my own purse, as you will learn from the certificate of the undertaker who made it.

BALTIMORE, *December 16, 1881.*

This is to certify that I made the coffin for the body of EDGAR ALLAN POE, and furnished the same by order of Dr. J. J. Moran, the resident physician of the Washington University Hospital, on Broadway, Baltimore City, for which he paid me out of his own pocket. I was employed as the undertaker for the institution during the time he had charge of the same, which was upward of six years. I made it out of poplar wood and stained it in imitation of walnut.

FREDERICK T. NEMUTH.
Undertaker.

Witness:
WILLIAM JAS. DEW.

My heart was in it. I furnished him the best nursing and attendance that the house could afford, and paid the hackman's fare who brought him; and up to this time I have not received a dime for it. I may be excused for being so specific in my statements. I do so to place myself properly before the public. It was not a charity hospital; my support depended alone upon the receipts of the house, and not one came forward to represent POE or to look after his welfare. He was sent there by some one unknown to me, and as yet unknown. The patients or their friends paid the usual charge in advance. But there was no one at that day to care for POE. He was friendless and penniless. Nor did any one ever pay a single

penny for his expenses while in my care.
Yet it gave me pleasure to have the distinguished poet in my charge, and I was proud
of the honor.

His body was laid in state in the large
room in the rotunda of the college building
adjoining the hospital, where it remained
from the 7th to the 9th of October. Hundreds of his acquaintances and friends came
to see him. At least fifty ladies received
a lock of his hair, the attendants waiting
upon them. It is generally received and
believed that he was brought to the hospital
in the night, and died before morning; and
it is reported to have been an unknown, out-
of-the-way hospital; that he was hid away
in the dark, visitors not being allowed to see
him, and was treated in all respects as a
poor castaway. A certain biographer has
recently written that "POE was four days in
a fit of delirium before he died;" and his
cousin, Nielson Poe, is reported by this same
writer to have said that he, Judge Poe, called
to see him, but he was in such wild delirium
that admission was refused; that he sent
changes of linen, etc., to add to his comfort.
I take this opportunity to assert that both
statements are utterly untrue and without
the slightest foundation.

Much has been said and written with regard to the great occasion of the dedication of the POE monument, on November 17, 1875, twenty-six years after the death of the poet, together with the names of the distinguished persons present, and who took part in the ceremonies, all of whom are justly entitled to much praise.

I desire to refer to a very touching incident that occurred at the time and which now comes to my mind with great force. At the tomb of the poet on that memorable occasion, when nearly all had left the sacred precinct now wrapped in silence, a venerable form, clothed in black and having the appearance of a prelate or minister in sacred things, was seen leaning upon the base of the shaft, apparently in deep devotion. The scene was most impressive, and the effect so decided upon the observer, who was a friend to the stranger, that he has put it in verse, several stanzas of which we give place to as a fitting memorial to the dead poet. The stranger was none other than Father Abraham J. Ryan, the poet-priest.

> A stranger stood beside a tomb,
> His manly form bent low,
> The tenant of the tomb, in life
> Was EDGAR ALLAN POE.

Was he a brother who had come,
  Fraternal tears to shed,
And with commingled love and pride
  Claim kin with the buried dead?

Or one, on whom, by chance the dead
  Had only simply smil'd,
Who now would turn aside the veil
  That hides this wayward child?

O, no! 'tis strange to say the stranger
  The sleeper never knew,
Though his tears have fallen in pearly chains,
  Like drops of " Hermon's dew."

But now! the Ritual is read,
  And the Requiem is sung,
At once by poet, priest and sage,
  With inspiration's tongue.

Hence, this tomb shall be an altar,
  Where slander once held feast,
And genius consecrated,
  Claims first the "poet-priest."

On October 9, 1849, when the body of POE
was consigned to the grave, the solemn and
impressive services, together with the names
of those present and the clergyman who
officiated, Rev. W. T. D. Clemm, were made
known to the public.   But a link has always
been wanting to make this part of POE'S history complete.   From whence was his body
taken? At what hour did it leave the hospital? Did any one feel sufficient interest in
the poet to follow his remains to the grave?

It is my privilege to furnish this link and to make this part of the poet's history complete. A hearse and hack were sent to the hospital for the body of POE. They arrived about 2.30 o'clock P. M. The body with the following attendants left the hospital at 3 o'clock: First among them was POE's most ardent admirer, Delosia Gill, Esq., brother of George M. Gill, Esq., Baltimore; then came Professor Dupey, teacher of French; Thos. Adams, president New York Life Insurance Company; Mr. Herring, a relative; Samuel Leakin, son of ex-Mayor Leakin; Dr. Thos. Tebbs, Dr. John Johns, the Drs. Dilliard, Dr. Brerwood, and Dr. Grey, from the institution and Virginia; George McCalpin, from Alabama; Dr. Wm. M. Cullen, Wm. Bishop, steward of the house; and I think Dr. Large, Dr. Taylor, and at least a dozen students of the college were in the funeral cortege.

The day was most unpleasant; a cold, cheerless one, accompanied by a cold, drizzly rain, nearly all day. Of the sympathizing friends and mourners present on the occasion, many were men of culture and of note; but of all those who composed the throng and mingled their tears over the dead, none bore in their hearts the poignant sorrow and grief of one who was absent, and the depth of whose tenderness and affection could not be estimated by mortal mind. I refer to the mother-in-law of the poet, Mrs. Maria Clemm.

Soon after his death, as requested by the poet, I communicated to this lady the sad intelligence, to which she replied in strains of the deepest sorrow, thanking me for the attention I had bestowed, as will be seen by reference to her letter now published in this volume.

The appearance of the dead poet had not materially changed; his face was calm and placid; a smile seemed to play around his mouth, and all who gazed upon him remarked how natural he looked; so much so, indeed, that it seemed as though he only slept.

Poe was a handsome man and was usually dressed in black. His head was exquisitely modelled; his forehead very prominent and largely developed, its measurement corresponding to that of Napoleon Bonaparte, a cast of which was then in my possession; his skin was fair; his hair was raven black and inclined to curl; his teeth were perfect; his eyes were brownish grey, large and full; his weight about 145 pounds; height, five feet ten inches; his hands were as delicate as a woman's. His whole appearance gave signs of the highest birth and pedigree.

Never shall we be permitted to look upon his equal again. He was one among the greatest of nature's poets, blessed with a transcendent genius above any of his contemporaries. He was a most affectionate husband and son. A kind and affectionate word from his wife or mother-in-law melted his sensitive nature to tears, and when his wife was buried, he spent whole nights in anguish at her grave. She was his dear "Lenore."

Unlike the Roman orator over the dead Caesar, we come to cast laurels at the grave of the distinguished dead poet, and to join the great throng in ascriptions of praise to his genius.

> Though cloud and shadow rest upon thy story,
> And rude hands lift the drapery of thy pall,
> Time as a birth-right, shall restore thy glory,
> And *truth* rekindle all the stars that fall.

I disparage my ability to express in fitting terms the marvelous gifts of this singular man. In the galaxy of great names that adorn the literature of our country, none is more radiant with the splendors of true

genius than that of POE. By the impartial
verdict of all fair-minded men, and by the
sober and dispassionate judgment of eminent
scholars and critics in both hemispheres,
the legacy of letters left to the world by this
child of song and sorrow entitles him to
the lasting gratitude of mankind, and the
crown of imperishable fame.

THE BELLS.

I.

Hear the sledges with the bells—
　　　Silver bells!
What a world of merriment their melody foretells!
　　How they tinkle, tinkle, tinkle,
　　　In the icy air of night!
　　While the stars that oversprinkle
　　All the heavens, seem to twinkle
　　　With a crystalline delight ;
　　Keeping time, time, time,
　　In a sort of Runic rhyme,
To the tintinnabulation that so musically wells
　　From the bells, bells, bells, bells,
　　　Bells, bells, bells—
From the jingling and the tinkling of the bells.

II.

　　Hear the mellow wedding bells,
　　　Golden bells,
What a world of happiness their harmony foretells!
　　Through the balmy air of night
　　How they ring out their delight !
　　　From the molten-golden notes,
　　　　And all in tune,
　　What a liquid ditty floats
To the turtle-dove that listens, while she gloats
　　　On the moon !
　　Oh, from out the sounding cells,
What a gush of euphony voluminously wells !
　　　How it swells !
　　　How it dwells
　　On the Future ! how it tells
　　Of the rapture that impels
　　To the swinging and the ringing
　　Of the bells, bells, bells,
　　Of the bells, bells, bells, bells,
　　　Bells, bells, bells—
To the rhyming and the chiming of the bells !

III.

Hear the loud alarum bells —
Brazen bells!
What a tale of terror, now, their turbulency tells!
In the startled ear of night
How they scream out their affright!
Too much horrified to speak,
They can only shriek, shriek,
Out of tune,
In a clamorous appealing to the mercy of the fire,
In a mad expostulation with the deaf and frantic fire,
Leaping higher, higher, higher,
With a desperate desire,
And a resolute endeavor
Now—now to sit or never,
By the side of the pale-faced moon.
Oh, the bells, bells, bells!
What a tale their terror tells
Of Despair!
How they clang, and clash, and roar!
What a horror they outpour
On the bosom of the palpitating air!
Yet the ear it fully knows,
By the twanging,
And the clanging,
How the danger ebbs and flows;
Yet the ear distinctly tells,
In the jangling,
And the wrangling,
How the danger sinks and swells,
By the sinking or the swelling in the anger of the bells—
Of the bells—
Of the bells, bells, bells, bells,
Bells, bells, bells —
In the clamor and the clangor of the bells!

IV.

Hear the tolling of the bells —
Iron bells!
What a world of solemn thought their monody compels!

In the silence of the night,
How we shiver with affright
At the melancholy menace of their tone!
For every sound that floats
From the rust within their throats
Is a groan.
And the people—ah, the people—
They that dwell up in the steeple,
All alone,
And who tolling, tolling, tolling,
In that muffled monotone,
Feel a glory in so rolling
On the human heart a stone—
They are neither man nor woman—
They are neither brute nor human—
They are Ghouls:
And their king it is who tolls;
And he rolls, rolls, rolls,
Rolls
A pæan from the bells!
And his merry bosom swells
With the pæan of the bells!
And he dances, and he yells;
Keeping time, time, time,
In a sort of Runic rhyme,
To the pæan of the bells—
Of the bells;
Keeping time, time, time,
In a sort of Runic rhyme,
To the throbbing of the bells—
Of the bells, bells, bells—
To the sobbing of the bells;
Keeping time, time, time,
As he knells, knells, knells,
In a happy Runic rhyme,
To the rolling of the bells—
Of the bells, bells, bells—
To the tolling of the bells,
Of the bells, bells, bells, bells—
Bells, bells, bells—
To the moaning and the groaning of the bells.